Stories of Fairytale Castles

Anna Lester

Illustrated by
Maria Cristina Lo Cascio

Reading Consultant: Alison Kelly
Roehampton University

Contents

Chapter 1

The invisible castle

Flora lived in a cottage on the edge of a forest. She spent all her time helping others.

She baked
bread and cakes
for the villagers...

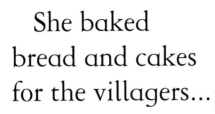

helped injured
animals...

and cheered
everyone up with
her funny stories.

One morning, Flora walked
deep into the forest. She was
on the hunt for juicy berries
for her cakes.

But as she looked, she left
the path. When she turned to
go home, Flora realized she
was lost.

Flora rushed through the forest in a panic. She didn't know which way to turn.

How will I ever get home?

Suddenly, she found herself in an enormous clearing. She ran across it...

and bumped straight into something. "Ow!" she cried. "What's that?"

7

Flora was puzzled. She could feel a cold, stone wall in front of her, but she couldn't see a single brick.

Flora felt along the wall with her hands until she found a gap and tried to go through. The next thing she knew, she had tripped up some invisible steps.

Flora scrambled to her feet. Now she was really curious. "Where do these steps go?" she wondered, and began to climb.

She went higher and higher, until she felt a wooden door. Flora pushed it open and gasped...

She could see a grand room
full of lords and ladies – each
of them frozen like icy statues.
Just then, a voice spoke.

Flora jumped. A young man stood in front of her.

"I didn't mean to frighten you," he said softly.

"I'm Prince Casper," he went on. "Welcome to my castle."

"What happened to everyone?" asked Flora.

"A witch cast a spell on them," said the Prince, sadly.

"They were guests at my ball," he explained, "but I didn't invite the witch, so she froze them."

Flora shivered.

"Then she made my castle walls invisible so no one could find me," Prince Casper added.

13

"Why didn't you go for help?" said Flora.

"I can't leave," the Prince sighed. "Watch!"

Prince Casper reached for the doorknob. As he touched it, his hand was stung by hundreds of icy crystals.

"You poor thing," cried Flora. She took his frozen hand and kissed it gently.

As she did so, the ice crystals melted away. Prince Casper was astonished.

At that moment, his guests
sprang to life and the
castle walls became
visible once more.

"The witch said only the
kindest girl in the kingdom
could break the spell," said the
Prince. "That must be you."

16

Flora was shocked. She was even more surprised when Prince Casper asked her to marry him.

The happy couple invited everyone to their wedding at the castle – including the local witches... just in case.

Chapter 2

The haunted castle

King Eric and Queen Ella lived in a beautiful castle, with twisting turrets and splendid rooms.

Servants waited on
them hand and foot.

And their son, Prince John,
was the most handsome man
in the land. There was just one
problem...

He wouldn't get married.
"What can we do?" said the
king. "He must marry *someone*."

"Let's invite the three
prettiest princesses to stay,"
said the queen. "He's sure to
fall in love with one of them."

The next day, Princesses Lily, Louisa and Lulu arrived. The servants watched them from a tower window.

"I wish I could be a princess," sighed Sally, the maid. "Then Prince John might marry me."

21

"I don't think that's likely, dear," said Clara the cook.

They crept downstairs, where the princesses were crowding around Prince John.

But, as soon as he left the room, their smiles vanished.

"I'm going to make sure he marries me," said Louisa. "I'm not letting this lovely castle slip through my fingers."

"Ha!" said Lily. "He'll choose me. I'm the prettiest."

"But I'm cleverer," laughed Lulu. "This castle's *mine*."

23

The servants were shocked.

"We can't let one of them marry the prince," said Sally. "They're only after the castle."

"Don't worry," said Clara. "I have a plan. Let's see how much they want to move into a *haunted* castle..."

That evening, Princess Lily had a nasty surprise when she climbed into bed...

...and Princess Louisa was
spooked on the stairs.

Then, in the middle of the night, Princess Lulu had a terrible fright.

Next morning, all three
princesses packed their bags.
"This castle is haunted,"
they said.

"We're never coming here
again. And none of us will
ever marry your son!"

"I'm afraid the princesses have left," the king told Prince John over breakfast.

"They think the castle is haunted," added the queen. "What nonsense!"

"Never mind," said Prince John, cheerfully. "I didn't want to marry any of them anyway." "Well, who *do* you want to marry?" demanded the king.

"If you must know, I want to marry Sally. And if I can't marry her, I'd rather not get married at all."

"You can't marry a maid!" shouted the king.

"She might be better than no one," whispered the queen. "I just need to be sure of her."

That evening, Sally went to the kitchen cupboard, as usual, to put away her things. But she opened it to see...

...a floating head with bright yellow eyes and a horrible, toothless grin.

"A real ghost!" screamed Sally, running from the room.

Not long after, she was
called to the throne room.

"I have something
to ask you," said
Prince John.

"Sally," he went on, getting
down on one knee. "Will you
marry me?"

"R-r-really? M-me?"
stammered Sally. "Yes please!"

"Even though the castle is haunted?" asked the king.

"Yes," said Sally, sounding sure, but turning a little green.

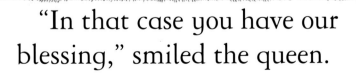

"In that case you have our blessing," smiled the queen.

34

Chapter 3

The castle contest

Once, a king and queen lived in a crumbling, tumble-down castle. It was musty and dusty and let in the rain.

We need a new home!

"We shall hold a contest!"
cried the king. "The
person who builds the
best castle will win
a chest of gold."

Everyone wanted to enter
the contest. The whole town
rushed to the castle
with their designs.

"I like the baker's design best," said the queen.

So the baker built his castle, with gingerbread bricks and toffee turrets.

It took him a month to build
and, when it was finished,
everyone gathered to see it.
"Amazing!" said the king.

As they admired the castle,
a bird swooped down and
pecked at the roof.
Soon, thousands of birds
were feasting on it...

Get off!

Hey!

...until there
were only
crumbs left.

The king sighed. "We'll hold *another* contest," he said, "with two chests of gold for the winner. But no food castles!"

Even more people came to the old castle, clutching ideas.

"I like the bookseller's design best," said the queen.

So, the bookseller
built his castle. It
had shining leather
walkways and a
paper roof.

It took him two months.
"Incredible!" said the king,
as a fat raindrop splashed on
his nose.

Another raindrop ran down the queen's gown. A crash of thunder shook the sky.

"Everyone into the castle!" shouted the king.

But the castle was already going soggy in the rain.

"What now?" asked the king, as he squished over the mushy floor.

"A third contest and *three* chests of gold?" suggested the queen.

This time, the queen liked the toymaker's design best. He began at once...

Is it ready yet?

...and worked behind an enormous curtain the whole time. "I like surprises," he said.

45

After three long months, the toymaker came to the throne room. "I've finished, your majesties!" he announced. And he showed them...

...a toy castle. The king stared at it. "Oh dear," he began.

The toymaker handed it to the queen. "For the castle nursery," he said, with a grin.
"Your real castle is outside."

The king and queen raced outside. "Perfect!" they cried together – and it was.

With thanks to Russell Punter,
Susanna Davidson and Lesley Sims

Designed by Hannah Ahmed

First published in 2007 by Usborne Publishing Ltd., Usborne House,
83-85 Saffron Hill, London EC1N 8RT, England. www.usborne.com
Copyright © 2007 Usborne Publishing Ltd.